The Hike

PRAISE FOR *STORYSHARES*

"One of the brightest innovators and game-changers in the education industry."
– Forbes

"Your success in applying research-validated practices to promote literacy serves as a valuable model for other organizations seeking to create evidence-based literacy programs."
- Library of Congress

"We need powerful social and educational innovation, and Storyshares is breaking new ground. The organization addresses critical problems facing our students and teachers. I am excited about the strategies it brings to the collective work of making sure every student has an equal chance in life."
– Teach For America

"Around the world, this is one of the up-and-coming trailblazers changing the landscape of literacy and education."
- International Literacy Association

"It's the perfect idea. There's really nothing like this. I mean wow, this will be a wonderful experience for young people."   - Andrea Davis Pinkney, Executive Director, Scholastic

"Reading for meaning opens opportunities for a lifetime of learning. Providing emerging readers with engaging texts that are designed to offer both challenges and support for each individual will improve their lives for years to come. Storyshares is a wonderful start."
- David Rose, Co-founder of CAST & UDL

The Hike

Jennie Ford

STORYSHARES

Story Share, Inc.
New York. Boston. Philadelphia

Storyshares
Story Share, Inc.
24 N. Bryn Mawr Avenue #340
Bryn Mawr, PA 19010-3304
www.storyshares.org

Inspiring reading with a new kind of book.

Interest Level: High School
Grade Level Equivalent: 3.7

9781973533849

Book design by Storyshares

Printed in the United States of America

Storyshares Presents

1

"It's broke, man."

"No, it isn't."

"It looks bad, dude."

"It's just a sprain."

"How do you know? You a freakin' doctor?!" Eric yelled.

"It's not swollen and black and stuff," Tom said.

"It is swollen. I see it!" Eric yelled again.

"Not like if it were broken. My brother broke his ankle in football. It swelled up like a balloon. It was black and blue and purple and nasty."

"Okay, guys, please shut up," I said. Tom and Eric looked at me. "Arguing isn't going to help. I don't know if it's broken or sprained, but boy . . . it hurts."

"Sprains are worse than breaks," Tom said.

"How do you know, stupid?" Eric asked.

"That's what I've heard, stupid!" Tom shot back.

"Guys, please! You're not helping. We gotta figure this out. It's a long way back," I said.

Tom and Eric thought about this.

"About three miles," Tom said.

"Are you kidding me?" Eric asked. "You're kidding me, right? More like, four or five miles, at least. We've been hiking for five hours."

"Not really," Tom said. "By the time we loaded everything and got ready, I'd say we hiked for maybe three hours."

Eric gave Tom a death stare. He looked like he was ready to explode. "You know everything, don't ya?" he finally asked.

Tom just shrugged his shoulders.

"I need you two to help me to the stream," I said.

The water in the mountain stream stayed ice cold, even in the dead of summer. Tom and Eric grabbed me under both arm pits and helped me hobble to the creek. They lowered me onto a rock to sit on. I took off my boot and sock, slowly. I stretched my leg and placed my poor ankle in the cold water. After a few minutes my whole foot felt numb and the pain eased.

"With your help, I think I can make it back to camp," I said.

"You think we should try to splint it"? Tom asked.

"With what? Did you die and come back as a wilderness survival expert?!" Eric yelled.

I looked at my watch. It was 4:15. It would get dark in about four hours . . . darker faster in the deep woods. We had to get going. "Let's do this." I said.

2

"We'll take turns carrying your back pack," Eric offered. "You first," he said, handing it to Tom.

"Figures," Tom muttered.

I found a small, sturdy branch and tried to use it like a cane. I limped slowly down the trail. My ankle was throbbing and felt hot. I was so stupid for allowing this to happen to me. I knew the rule of hiking was to never step on a rock or a log unless you tested it first to make sure it was sturdy and secure. I had been too excited to get to the end of the trail. There, we would come upon the great

Bridal Veil Falls. I had only seen pictures of it, and it had looked amazing.

In my haste, I'd stepped on a large rock. It had been loose and rolled. My foot became caught between it and another large rock. I went down hard. Eric and Tom were able to move the rock enough for me to remove my wedged foot. That's when the pain had hit.

Eric and Tom had both looked at me with concerned and confused expressions. I knew they must have been wondering how I could make such an amateur mistake.

I wondered it too.

This was on me.

We then walked, or they walked, at least, while I hobbled and limped for what seemed like hours. Really, it was only thirty minutes. The pain in my ankle became too great at that point, and I told them that I had to sit down. It was 4:45. I knew we had to keep going. We couldn't be stuck out here in the dark.

"One of you is going to have to go ahead and get help," I said. "I'm holding us up. I don't want all of us stuck out here at night. We can't make this trail in the dark. Too risky."

"I'll go," Eric said. "You and Tom keep moving as much as you can. I'll bring back help."

For once, Tom didn't argue with him.

"Okay, Eric, be safe," I said. "I'm sorry about all this."

"It's cool," Eric said.

"See ya in a little while," Tom said.

"You will," Eric said and started down the trail.

Tom let me lean on him with my arm around his neck. The trail was starting to slope downward and was getting quite steep. We came around a bend to where the fast-moving stream was parallel to the trail.

"I think you should soak your foot a bit," Tom said.

"Good idea," I said.

We made our way down a small bank to the water's edge. I sat and let the icy water soothe my ankle. Tom sat beside me, throwing pebbles in the stream. The water was so clear. We could see the pink streaks of the rainbow trout as they swam by, glinting in the lowering sun.

Tom looked deep in thought. "You know," he said,"I've never known anyone who has actually seen Bridal Veil Falls. Sure, everyone's heard of it, but I don't know anyone who's seen it. Not even my Dad. He wasn't even sure how to find the falls, and he knows everything about these mountains. Do you know anyone who's seen them?" he asked.

"Come to think of it, I don't," I said. "I've seen pictures of them."

"How did you find this camp, Wyatt?" Tom asked.

"Actually, I found a map for this camp in an old atlas at my Grandpa's hunting cabin. I've got it with me. Let me see my pack."

Tom handed over the heavy pack, and I pulled the map out of a side pocket. The paper it was scrawled on was yellowed with age.

"See, there's old Highway 50. There's the logging camp road that we took. Here's the place we veered off, by the old Henson place. Remember passing it?" I asked Tom.

"That old, broke-down, haunted-looking house? I remember," he said.

"Here's the X for the camp. We sure found it," I said.

"Yes, we did," Tom said and took the wrinkled bit of paper from me. "Look, it's faded, but here on the bottom, it says something," Tom strained his eyes. "It says, *Property of Eldread Frizzell.* It says something else . . . but it's so faded." Tom held the paper up to the sunlight. "It says, *Damned . . .* What the hell is that supposed to mean?" Tom asked.

3

"Eldread," I said, "That was the name of the old man we met coming in today. Must be his grandfather or father who owned this land."

It seemed like days ago but was only this morning when we pulled into the remote camp. We'd ridden a couple miles on what looked to be a cattle path of grass and dips and rocks. Dad's old hunting truck had squeaked loudly at every dip and bump. There wasn't really a sign to announce that we had arrived. Instead, the road had ended at a small wooded plot.

We'd slowed and driven in.

The first campsite we came upon, we found a man sitting in a rocker whittling a chunk of wood. An old hound dog lay at his feet. He'd worn faded denim overalls and heavy black work boots.

It would be difficult to guess his age because of the thick gray beard that had hung down to his chest. It'd masked his features to where all you could see were his coal eyes and ample nose. He'd been a big man. Not fat. The kind of big a man gets from hard work. He was broad and tall.

He waved to us, so we'd felt obliged to say hello. He'd stood but didn't walk to the truck. He spoke loudly from a small distance. "Howdy," he had said. "Where you boys from?"

"Just down the mountain, in Bethel," I had answered him.

"I'm Dread, Eldread, but people call me Dread, and this here is Sheba," he said, pointing to the hound.

I answered him with polite words and a smile.

"A great night for camping. Full moon. You boys be careful out there. Them woods are dark and deep."

"Yes, sir, we will. Thank you," I said.

We drove past him, and Eric said something to the effect that his type is what gives us mountain people a bad name. "He looks like something straight out of a movie about dumb hillbillies," he said.

The next campers we had encountered were a couple, probably in their twenties. They sat in fold out camping chairs. The man was preoccupied with tying a fishing lure, and the lady sat swatting at gnats. They didn't seem to notice us drive by.

The road curved, and we saw another campsite. A well-tanned middle-aged man sat in a small hammock. He wore sunglasses and gave a rather creepy grin as we drove by. His camp looked as if he had been there a while. He had cooking pots hanging over his fire, a clothes line, and an ample stack of wood. We had drove past him to find a more secluded spot.

The Hike

4

"How's it feeling, Wyatt?" Tom asked.

"Better. Let's get moving," I said.

Tom was helping me up from my perch by the stream when we heard a loud snap of a branch. We both stood still and heard more branches breaking and a loud tramping noise. It was as if someone was running fast, breaking through the brush.

"What is that?" we both asked.

"Wait here," Tom said. He took off toward the noise. I could hear his footsteps running down the trail. Then, I heard his footsteps running back. Fast.

"You gotta see this," he said, catching his breath.

I grabbed my walking stick, and put my arm around his neck.

"Oh, man. Oh, man," Tom kept saying.

"Slow down a bit, Tom. I can't walk this fast," I told him. The path was all downhill now and scattered with rocks.

We made it to a large hemlock tree that sat directly beside the trail. "Look!" Tom said, pointing to the side of the tree facing us. "Look!" he said again.

I hopped closer to him and saw what he was pointing at. The tree was carved with three stick figures. The third stick figure had a deep carved X over it, leaving two.

I ran my fingers over the carved figures. It felt wet and sticky. It was newly done. The deep grooved X oozed thick, sticky sap.

There had to be a logical explanation, but my mind went blank. *Somebody is pranking us . . . has to be*, I thought.

"Who did this?" Tom asked. "This is messed up, Wyatt. Totally messed up."

"We gotta get out of here," I said. "No more stopping. Something's wrong."

5

It was now 5:53, and already the forest looked darker. The sky, what I could see of it through the thick, tall trees, was filling with gray clouds. The wind was picking up. I had checked the weather before we left home, and there was no mention of rain. But in the mountains, anything was possible.

We made our way slowly. I used my stick, and Tom held me up as much as he could. We came around a bend and stopped dead in our tracks. Tom pointed, but I had already seen. Eric's back pack was hanging off a low branch. It hung right in the middle of the trail.

"NO. NO. NO," was all that Tom could say.

I stood there and watched the pack swing back and forth in front of me. I tried to think logically, but, again, I couldn't. I needed to think of a reason as to why the backpack was here.

I looked at my watch. It was 6:19. The thick forest was getting darker. The sky was getting more gray. I started to tremble.

Tom cautiously walked to the pack and pulled it loose. He sat on his knees and opened it up.

"Looks like everything is still in here," Tom said. "Maybe he left it for us in case we needed it."

"But who made the noises? Who carved the tree?" I asked.

Tom looked at me. He too was trying to think of something logical. "Let's keep going," he said.

We kept going. We were quiet. Our minds raced with unanswered questions and fear.

"It's getting dark. Rain?" Tom asked.

"Don't know," I said.

6

We trudged slowly on. The sky was getting black, and we heard thunder rumbling through the mountains. The wind began to blow harder, and the trees began to sway. The wind in the mountains could play tricks on you. It would sound like a heavy wave barreling toward you or like a wolf howling through the valley.

Tom stopped walking. "Listen," he whispered.

We heard a heavy-footed walk. It had a steady and determined pace. We listened. *Is it coming towards us or moving away from us? Is it someone to help us or hurt us? Do we hide or yell for help?*

"It's getting louder. It's coming this way," Tom said quietly.

"Hide," I said. We found a thick stand of mountain laurel trees. We crawled inside the thick leaves and low-lying branches. We settled ourselves on our bellies and looked to the trail.

The heavy steps were getting closer. We couldn't see the trail clearly, but we could hear. Tom put his hand over his mouth to silence his scared, heavy breath. The footsteps were right at us now. I peeked through the branches to see but only saw boots: black, heavy work boots. They walked slowly on the trail right in front of our hiding place. They stopped. They turned around.

Whoever was wearing those boots was searching . . . searching for us. If he was looking for us to help us, he would be yelling our names. He would have others with him. He wasn't here to help us. I knew that now.

The boots turned again and pointed right at us. We froze. I thought that the branches surrounding me must surely be shaking because my whole body was, and I couldn't stop it.

The boots walked toward our hiding place and stopped. He finally turned and went up the trail to where we had come from.

Tom still had his hand over his mouth, and his eyes were shut tight. I nudged him.

"Tom, breathe," I mouthed. He took his hand away and quietly caught his breath.

"What do we do?" he silently mouthed back. I shook my head. I didn't know.

We could stay put and quietly wait it out. Our parents wouldn't get worried until late tomorrow when we didn't arrive home. Too long, way too long. Maybe the other campers would notice that we never came out of the woods, and they'd call a Ranger. Maybe Eric made it. Eric. I couldn't think about him right now.

I nudged Tom again. He looked to me.

"We hide," I said, oh so softly.

7

The rain came. It started with a few large drops. Then it came with all its might. It poured. The thunder clapped, and the lightning flashed. The downpour caused the water to flow from the trail to where we lay like small rivers, soaking us to the bone. Soon, we were covered in mud, pine needles, and leaves.

I looked up to the sky, and the wind blew the white flowers from the laurel in the air like confetti. I watched as they danced in the wind.

The full moon occasionally peeked out from behind the thick clouds and lit up the tops of the tall trees. I felt hot tears run down my face. I wanted my Mama.

Tom nudged me hard. I looked to him, and he pointed to the trail. The boots were back. This time, they turned and went into the woods opposite of us. We listened for how far they might have went into the woods.

The wind and rain made it impossible to hear. My immediate thought was that the boots knew we were here, and they were sitting across from us, waiting us out.

It was 8:00 and pitch black. The storm subsided, but a steady rain poured down. All I could see was Tom's form laying beside me, and all I could hear was his stifled breath.

And then . . . a light? I caught a small bobbing light in the corner of my eye. I slowly moved my head to look down the trail in its direction. Tom saw it too and craned his head to look at it. It was a flashlight moving up the trail.

"Wyatt! Tom!"

It was Eric! Thank God! It was Eric! Oh no, the boots, the man! My mind was racing.

"I'm going," Tom said. I grabbed at his arm, but it was too late. He was up. He jumped around on his legs that were cramped and numb from lying still for too long, and then he ran.

That's when the heavy boots hit the trail so hard that rocks flew in my face. He had been waiting us out, perched on the bank opposite of us.

"Eric! Help!" I heard Tom scream as he ran down the trail. He was frantic. And then I heard a growl. It wasn't like a bear or a mountain lion. The only growl that would come close to it would be a tiger. A deep, loud, menacing growl. It echoed through the forest.

"HELP! HELP!" Tom screamed in a voice that wasn't his. It was the voice of terror.

Everything grew quiet, too quiet. The growling stopped. Tom wasn't screaming anymore.

I wiped my tears and found a flower petal stuck to my face. I peeled it off. It felt soft. I held it in my hand.

The bushes that had become my sanctuary parted and an old hound stuck her nose in.

"Boy? You in there?" It was Dread. He held his flashlight and shined it in my face. "Well you're just dug in here like a groundhog, ain't cha?" he said. He set the flashlight on the ground and reached out to me. The light shone on his old black work boots. I looked at the hand he offered. His fingernails were long and black. My eyes grew big. He grinned at me. His teeth were like an animal's, long and sharp.

My heart raced, and I couldn't catch my breath. He threw his head back and howled. The howl turned into a growl. The tiger growl. The monster growl.

And then there was darkness.

Epilogue

"Is this it Dad?"

"Should be."

We pulled into the old camp ground. Dad slowed the SUV to talk to an old man who sat in a rocker. He had a hound sleeping at his feet.

The old man waved. "Howdy folks."

"Hello," Dad said. "I'm hoping we have the right place. Is this where the trail head is for Bridal Veil Falls?" he asked.

"It sho is," the old man said. "My name is Eldread, but people call me Dread."

"Good to meet you," we both said.

"A great night for camping. Full moon. You folks be careful out there, ya hear? Those woods are dark and deep."

"We will. Thank you," Dad said. "What a character," Dad said to me and grinned as we pulled away.

We continued on the bumpy path. We passed a young couple. The man was busy tying a fishing lure and the lady sat in a fold out chair swatting at gnats. We rounded a bend and noticed an older man. He wore sunglasses and sat in a hammock. He grinned as we rode past. Dad waved.

"Let's find a more secluded spot," Dad said. "There's a good site, but it's taken. We'll go a little further."

I looked out my open window and saw three teen boys sitting around a fire pit that had no fire. "They look odd," I said.

"They're probably just tired from hiking," Dad said.

"Probably so," I said.

The Hike

About The Author

Jennie Ford is a mother, writer, potter, and artist. Jennie was raised in eastern North Carolina, where the rich farming landscapes provide the backdrop to many of her stories.

As a contributor to Storyshares for many years, she will continue to compose short stories for their expanding library. Now residing in western North Carolina, Jennie is currently writing a novel for young adult readers, which she hopes to publish in the future.

According to Jennie, "The goals of the Storyshares organization are wonderful and much needed." Jennie continues to feel pride lending her

talents to the benefit of struggling and beginning readers with age-appropriate
and thoughtful stories. She is excited to learn that her stories may instill the love of reading in many.

About The Publisher

Story Shares is a nonprofit focused on supporting the millions of teens and adults who struggle with reading by creating a new shelf in the library specifically for them. The ever-growing collection features content that is compelling and culturally relevant for teens and adults, yet still readable at a range of lower reading levels.

Story Shares generates content by engaging deeply with writers, bringing together a community to create this new kind of book. With more intriguing and approachable stories to choose from, the teens and adults who have fallen behind are improving their skills and beginning to discover the joy of reading. For more information, visit storyshares.org.

Easy to Read. Hard to Put Down.

Made in the USA
Middletown, DE
20 January 2023

22532531R00028